Breakfast
with Jackie O.

and other short stories

Burt Jagolinzer

Breakfast with Jackie O.
and other short stories

by

Burt Jagolinzer

Visit our website at **www.StillwaterPress.com** for more information.

First Stillwater River Publications Edition

ISBN-10: 0-997-87785-5
ISBN-13: 978-0-997-87785-4
Library of Congress Control Number: 2016946289

1 2 3 4 5 6 7 8 9 10
Written by Burt Jagolinzer
Cover Design by Dawn M. Porter
Published by Stillwater River Publications, Glocester, RI, USA.
All images and graphics used in this book are in the public domain.

Dedication

This book is dedicated to my love for:

My significant other, Nancy Parenti

My brother and his wife, Ken and Ruthie Jagolinzer

My daughters, Cheryl Marcus and Wendy Segal

My grandchildren, Caroline Marcus, Zach Marcus
and Jacob Segal

Acknowledgements

The author gratefully acknowledges:

Jennifer Wells for initial proof-reading

Dawn and Steven Porter of Stillwater River Publications

And Almighty God, who in his infinite way has made all this possible.

Table of Contents

Breakfast with Jackie O.

Ralphie Bosko was a plumber. His father was a plumber. Ralph Sr. had trained his son to be the best that a plumber could be.

They were extremely proud of Ralphie and his special abilities in the family trade.

Ralph Sr. had escaped East Berlin, Germany months after the Berlin Wall had been erected in 1961. He had crossed into the West at night with a group of five.

One of them had been killed by border control at the crossing, another one took a bullet in the back.

Ralph Sr. was lucky to have made it unscathed.

A month later, he met up with his childhood sweetheart, Nina, who had bribed her way across the border to Ralph's waiting arms.

Soon they were able to find a working arrangement to sail to America.

Their ship arrived in New Jersey. Someone recommended jobs in the Washington, D.C. area.

He took the first job he was offered. It was working with a plumber who was employed by a large construction firm. His apprenticeship lasted almost two years. He was let go.

Ralph began putting his new found skills to use on his own. Word got around the community that a new skilled plumber was available.

His business began to grow. He worked cheaply and his clients appreciated it. Ralph became popular and his income afforded him to easily support his growing family.

His son Ralphie was to pick up on the skills that he needed to follow into his father's successful business. And it wasn't long before his father began turning the work over to his son.

Ralphie settled in the Greater Washington, D.C. area.

He adjusted the business to focus on "home service" for fast lucrative income. He envisioned a "business belt" large enough to hold his challenge for the future.

And so he began servicing the District of Columbia and the surrounding communities.

His first call came from the condominium of Senator Abraham Silk, Democrat from Alaska, whose kitchen sink was clogged.

Mrs. Silk had a backup drain with dishes piled in the sink. Ralphie took out the dirty dishes and plunged the water drain.

The water cleared and he cleaned the area. Before leaving, he applied a chemical absorber that would loosen any clogging that may have caused the backup.

He received a check from Mrs. Silk for sixty dollars. She also honored him with a ten-dollar cash tip, "for keeping it clean."

Adriane Moss had a toilet clogged and was unable to flush again. She had tried to use a plunger but to no avail. Ralphie quickly came to the rescue.

He found that the lifting valve was worn and needed replacement. He also snaked the drain to allow the refuse to work its way out properly.

Within thirty minutes, he had replaced the worn valve and cleaned everything up.

Mrs. Moss gave Ralphie seventy-five dollars in cash and a cold cola for his excellent effort.

Ralphie worked this way for nearly twenty years.

He serviced businesses, the homes of businessmen, the homes of congressmen, condominiums, townhouses, and apartments throughout the area.

One day he got a telephone call from the Georgetown section.

He was told that there was a leak in a dishwasher that could not be found or stopped.

When he arrived and the door opened, he came face-to-face with Jackie Onassis. He couldn't believe it.

"Are you Jackie O?" he asked.

"Yes," she responded. "Please don't make much of it. My kitchen washer leaks and I need your help."

Within ten minutes, he had found the culprit. It was a copper tube connecting running water to the washer itself.

He went back to his truck and returned with his propane torch and some solder. Quickly he began to heat and solder the leaky connection. Jackie asked him if he'd had breakfast. "No, only a cup of coffee about an hour ago," he replied.

"Good. I'll make you some breakfast and we'll eat together."

"Wow!" was his response.

He finished the patch-up job on the washer connector. The smell of French toast and bacon was overtaking him. He was now ready for breakfast.

"Just sit down here, next to me," she requested.

"There's coffee and juice if you like... and help yourself to the toast and bacon."

Ralphie did help himself to this wonderful offering. He couldn't believe what was happening.

The food was terrific and Jackie's table talk made it special and unusual.

Jackie asked him if he had ever visited Cape Cod, in Massachusetts or Newport, Rhode Island where important parts of her life had taken place.

"No, I have not visited either place, but I've read quite a lot about both areas and would love to get to visit them sometime soon," he answered.

"If you ever plan to visit these locales, I invite you to telephone my personal travel guru, Elizabeth Cogan in New York City, who will gladly make plans for you. All my friends, family and professional visitors use her. Just tell her that I told you to treat you in a special manner. Here is one of her cards. In fact, I insist that she give you my personal discount and I will tell her so next week when I get ready to travel to California."

"I don't know what to say. You have given me an excellent breakfast, wonderful discussion, and now access to your personal travel connections. I don't think I deserve such favor."

"I can't charge you for the service that I just performed," he countered.

Jackie quickly responded. "Oh yes, I must pay you for your quick and excellent work. Please don't mix the other offers in that matter. I need to know the charge for your service now."

"It would be a minimum $70 charge… but I still don't think it is fair for you to pay it."

She immediately paid him the seventy dollars in cash.

He shook his head in disbelief and gathered his equipment and jacket before saying goodbye.

When he packed his truck with the equipment, he continued to shake his head in disbelieve at all that had just happened.

He serviced two other jobs that day but couldn't get the morning event out of his mind.

At the end of the work day, he drove home.

After opening his front door, he took off his trusty jacket. Next he emptied his two front pockets which housed the paper receipts and miscellany of the day's work.

To his surprise, the right side pocket had an additional plastic item.

When he examined it he discovered a rolled-up paper sticking out of a small plastic tube. He quickly unrolled the paper item and found a hand-written note from Jackie. It read:

Nice people deserve encouragement.

-- Jacqueline Bouvier-Kennedy-Onassis

"Wow. I can't believe it!" he exclaimed.

And inside the plastic tube was an uncirculated Kennedy fifty-cent coin.

He proudly told his story to all his friends, relatives and any clients who would listen.

He had the note from Jackie professionally framed and mounted it above Ralphie's own bed, along with the uncirculated coin.

He would tell those interested, "having had breakfast with Jackie O, I am now ready to have lunch with Bugs Bunny or the President of the United States."

Alexander's Ragtime Band

ome on and hear. *Come on and hear.*

Peter Alexander began forming an upbeat social band.

He decided to place an ad in his local New Orleans newspaper to locate local, gifted performers.

Ronnie Hupendozer was among the first to answer his ad. Hupendozer had played b-flat tuba in the US Navy Band and had just completed his service to the nation.

Ronnie wanted a chance to audition for Alexander. He was told to come by on Wednesday at 9 a.m. for that opportunity.

Alfred Goofoffer arrived with his mother. Alfred was just fifteen years-old but had been performing with the New Orleans New Jazz Company on his trusty clarinet. He had his instrument with him, but it needed a replacement reed and a key was sticking quite badly. He begged for another audition time.

Alexander committed to Wednesday as well, assigning 10 a.m. for his audition.

Sally Swiftberger arrived with her harmonica. Alexander immediately told her that her instrument wouldn't meet his requirements. She left in a huff.

The next person to walk into Alexander's room was Norman Clements at six-foot-ten inches tall. He scraped the door entrance, barely making it through the opening. He was built thin and looked fragile.

"I play a mean alto sax and sing like a gazelle," he explained.

"Gazelle's don't sing the last I knew," Alexander responded.

"I'm a fast singer like a gazelle, and I learn songs that way as well," the giant countered.

"We don't need a gazelle... but if you can play alto like you say, then I will schedule you for an audition on Wednesday at 1 p.m.," Alexander responded.

"OK. I'd like the opportunity to do just that." The big guy turned to attempt to leave the room and once again barely made it through the doorway.

Responses to the ad continued throughout that Monday. Some twenty-three individuals came for an interview.

Peter's Wednesday was completely booked with auditions. He was amazed at the variety of musicians who had come to meet with him. He hoped to hire about ten to fill his ragtime band.

Wednesday couldn't come soon enough for Peter Alexander.

Peter used Tuesday to prepare his musical arrangements.

On Wednesday, he was ready to hand-pick some talent to fill his immediate needs as a big band.

He selected three saxophones -- two were tenors and one was alto. The big guy who had hardly made it into his audition room was the alto.

The other two had played around town in various pubs and restaurants. Two trumpet players were chosen. Each played flugal and trumpet and had enough of a background to meet Peter's standards.

In came Herman Clopper a jazz drummer who had the latest equipment and experience. He had been playing three nights a week on Basin Street. The pay was not good and he wanted a better overall arrangement. Peter promised him just that.

Dustin Grey played Trombone as his late cousin Al had done. He was taught by Al and could actually imitate many of Al's special gestures. His sound was terrific and he read music quite well.

Jennifer Purdue claimed the female vocalist position. She had a steady gig at Poppy's on Parade Street in the French Quarter. Her mother had toured with Oscar Bromley back in the 80's. She sang very much like Carmen McRey.

Rodney Bissette was hired as male vocalist. Rod had performed in five Hollywood motion pictures. His voice was very original and his sound captured attention by most listeners.

Ronnie Hupendozer and his b-flat tuba were also added to this classic entourage.

John "Dapper" McClain became the pianist for the group. This gifted musician had played with Tommy Dorsey's uncle, Bill Dorsey in Dallas, Texas for the last twenty years. Bill Dorsey had passed away at age 89 and the band had broken up.

The timing for the forming of this group was excellent.

Pete Alexander was ready to go.

The Ragtime band was advertised throughout New Orleans and business opportunities were beginning to arrive.

Their first gig was aboard the *Magellin,* a cruise ship at dockside.

The ownership had several other ships and decided to hire their band to work on the international *Sea-Span,* an ocean-going vessel loaded with vacationing individuals.

The *Sea-Span* kept this musical group together riding the Atlantic Ocean and the islands.

Their lives were all aboard ship. But they were paid quite well and the tips were even better. These guys were making plenty of money.

And because their money was made in international waters... no taxes were demanded.

During the Second World War their ship disappeared. It had been captured by the Russians. There were a total 142 on board at the time.

The Premier of Russia, Josef Stalin, decided not to tell anyone about the hijacking. Instead he shipped the vessel and its people to Siberia, under lock and key.

The individuals on board were accommodated new lives and the band kept playing regularly for Soviet elite. They received their pay in Russian currency.

Peter Alexander became a Russian hero. He learned the language and even married a local girl, Consondra Plurr. They had two children.

Their son, Muri became a major in the Russian Army. Alexandra was a model for women's fashions in Moscow.

The members of the band (who saved all their dollars paid to them aboard ship before the take-over) converted their savings to Russian funds and lived high in the Siberian suburbs.

Several of them found companions among the locals and lived happily ever after.

The United States never found out the true story. Many thought they had disappeared into the Bermuda Triangle.

It is interesting to note that the families of those on board never were able to find a link to this happening. They faced finality and accepted their losses.

In Josef Stalin's memoirs, he tells of the many slaughters of key people around him. He mentions the capture of the *Sea-Span* and gives some indication that other captures and eliminations of his enemies and their associates took place.

Japan, Germany and Great Britain have talked about disappearances during the time of World War Two and the reign of Josef Stalin.

He was truly ruthless and many other atrocities could have occurred involving the Russian's reign of power.

No one today can document any of these possibilities. The world will probably never know what else Stalin might have done.

Certainly a moral of this story is that the Siberian Russians luckily enjoyed the wonderful music of our "Alexander's Ragtime Band."

"Ants in Your Pants" Are Good for Your Health

The Hubercaci Ant, found at the edge of eastern Mongolia, has been found to be good for your health.

According to the Mongolian National Health Magazine (printed in China monthly) the Hubercaci Ant is loaded with cure bionics that soften material, especially cotton, and other miscellaneous mixed fabrics.

This softness provides more comfort for your average pants. It also increases the stability and length of wear, time. The unusual softness is believed to help individuals to want-to "keep their pants on."

It is believed that this softness can also eliminate chafing and the loss of comfort usually found in store-bought pants.

Additional health improvement factors are scheduled to be released by the reporting authorities during the next two years.

The Hubercaci Ant is expected to be imported to America (and to England) shortly. Distribution centers will be placed in Boston, New York, Cleveland, Denver and Los Angeles.

The future will undoubtedly prove that it is better to have "ants in your pants" than have "sugar in your tea."

Stock Market: Hubercaci Ant (HA) can be found "Over the Counter", currently at $12 per share.

I Bought a Locker
at the Self-Storage Auction

It was two days after Christmas. The auction had been advertised for several weeks.

My buddy, Albert Solo, had been planning to go. He had been working on me to accompany him. It was not something that I would have gone out of my way to do, but being a friend of Albert and having the free-time, I decided to go along with him.

We arrived at the self-storage building just before twelve. The auction was to start at noon. The place was very crowded. Mostly men were present.

And it was cold. The temperature was only about twenty degrees. We were all bundled up.

The Auctioneer was a tall, slender guy, about fifty years-old. He wore a brown wide-brim dress hat and he held his trusty clip-board close to his chest. A microphone was prepared in front of his small desk which was on wheels.

Albert and I stood almost at the back of the fenced-in yard that housed the brick building which had been custom-built to contain large and small lockers for client renters.

Tom, the Auctioneer, introduced himself and began to state the rules and regulations involved in the auction program. He stated that the contents of 71 lockers were to be auctioned off.

Albert told me that last year he bought the contents of a small locker for $15. Among the junk in the locker, he found a camera (which he eventually sold at a local flea market for $35, a small television (that he gave to his niece Carla), three six-packs of light beer, and a pair of brand-new white athletic socks.

Obviously Albert thought it was well worth his investment and enjoyed the fun that came with it.

The Auctioneer stated that "everything was to be sold "AS IS" without recourse." He then described the first locker to be sold.

He stated that this large locker was rented by a master mechanic who had left town in a hurry. It had been untouched for well over a year.

The bid started at $5 and quickly went to $25. Finally, a youngster bought it at $45.

The second small locker belonged to a school teacher who had eloped with a minister at her church. (It had become popular local gossip). It too had not been touched for over a year.

Albert raised his hand to start the bidding at $5. No one else bid on it. The auctioneer didn't waste time. He awarded the bid to Albert.

Albert was elated. He couldn't wait to see what he bought. The rules prohibited anyone from opening their purchased lockers until the auction was completed.

Locker number seven was next. It was another large one. It had belonged to a farmer, who had died and his family showed no interest in paying the past-due rent and retrieving whatever had been stored inside. It was at least a year since anyone had visited this locker.

The guy next to me raised his hand and started the bid at $25. Three other men and one woman continued bidding until the price had risen to over $100.

The guy next to me finally won the bid at $105. He immediately left the bidder's group. Albert and I wondered what could have been in that locker?

Locker fourteen was the next to be auctioned. There were two English racer-type bikes attached to the large door. They were to be included in this bid.

Albert started the bid at $10. Someone in the front immediately bid $100. Two others pushed the bid to $200. The person in the front ended up winning the bid at $390. Wow!

Large locker seventeen was next. It had been rented by a lawyer who had been going through a divorce. The lawyer appeared to have left town without paying the year's rent that was due.

I started the bid at $10. Several people continued to push the price to $100. I quickly bid $110. To my surprise, the auctioneer awarded me the locker.

Albert said it was time to leave the auction, and get a cup of coffee, until the auction became completed.

We walked to the nearby doughnut shop. There, we talked about our purchases and joked about the possible junk we might have procured.

About an hour later the auction appeared to have ended. We left the doughnut shop and walked to the auctioneer's office to pay our bills. An employee walked us to our lockers and opened the doors.

I decided to go with Albert to his locker first. We entered and turned on the lights.

The contents had belonged to a school teacher. It was loaded with books, college class materials, text books and romance novels of all sorts.

Among the books was an old wardrobe chest with draws. The top drawer was loaded with mail. It appeared they were love letters from past relationships.

The second drawer had pictures and photos of her family, friends and apparent romantic acquaintances. Other junk filled the corners of the drawer.

The third drawer had a collection of coins and some small packages of stamps (of possible value).

Other used items crammed into the locker included a beat-up toilet seat, a painted stepstool and a broken window.

Albert laughed and I smiled back at him. He said he would make the most of what was there. He appeared satisfied.

We moved on to my locker.

As we opened the door a smell from within caught us it was not good. The odor had an egg-type whiff. What were we about to get into?

I remembered that this locker had been rented by a lawyer.

The entrance was blocked by a sit-down lawn tractor. It appeared to be in new condition. I figured this piece must be worth a bunch of money.

Albert and I pushed the tractor out into the corridor to give us access to the interior.

There were boxes piled upon boxes. I spotted a tall lamp in the right corner. The left corner had automobile tires stacked to the ceiling. They appeared to be new. Financially, I felt that I was already ahead.

The first box that we opened was filled with tax returns. The name on the copies was John Durham Smith, Esquire. There were some ten years of returns within the box. We put it aside and picked-up the second box.

In this box we found a large series of government bonds, dating from 1979 to 2007. Wow. There must have been several thousands of dollars in this box. I'd hit a bonanza.

I couldn't put the box down. I held on to it tightly.

Albert opened the third box and found stacks of comic books. They too were old (circa 1970). I was sure they must have value to a collector.

I finally put the bond box down next to my feet and began opening another box.

It was full of broken jewelry, watches, earrings, broaches and cuff-links. I thought that they might contain some diamonds, gold and silver of decent monetary value.

Among the jewelry was a small ring case. Within the case was a note, stating that this diamond ring belonged to a sister Laurene, who had acquired it during her failed marriage to Paul Longsleeve. The diamond ring had been appraised three years ago at $9,000.

Now I had two boxes to protect.

Albert uncovered a box full of expense receipts dating back to 1973.

My next box had a letter from the lawyer's mother and her picture posing with another woman. Several neckties filled the rest of the box.

Albert had already opened the next box. He found ledgers from the lawyer's personal legal practice, dating back at least ten years.

The next box had written on the outside face, "Safety Deposit Info." It contained an envelope with two keys, but the location of the safety deposit material was not there.

We went through the enclosed papers. They indicated that fees for maintaining the rental space had been paid for several years. The receipts did not indicate where the location was either.

It appeared that we had reached an end of any possibility of locating the boxes when it dawned on me that maybe the two keys would help locate where this material may have been stored or still remained.

I returned to the envelope and procured the two keys.

Sure enough on the key slot was engraved, "Sterling Hotel."

I called information on my phone and they had no information for a Sterling Hotel.

I decided to telephone the police, to see if they could help me find the hotel.

Captain Seymour Hoover returned my call about forty-minutes later.

He had located the hotel, about one hundred miles away in New Hampshire. I told him about my purchase and the notation on the box containing the keys.

I asked him whether he could assign someone to visit the hotel with me. He said that he would appoint his assistant, Private Maxwell Roche.

His assistant and I traveled to the Sterling Hotel. They quickly identified the number 54 on the key and directed us to a safety deposit box with that number. One of the keys immediately opened the small rental box.

The box was loaded with hundred dollar bills (many thousands of dollars). Also in the box was a 45-caliber pistol and a full magazine of ammunition.

Private Maxwell Roche stepped forward and demanded to take control of the whole box. "We will see where this stash leads us," he stated. "Let's go back to Headquarters."

Within a couple of hours, the police had determined the ownership of the gun. It belonged to a doctor, who had reported it taken, along with several other items, about a week ago.

The hundred dollar bills had been traced to a bank robbery in the next state, about four months ago. Three robbers had been killed and one had escaped.

It appeared that the escaped robber hid the money and had not been discovered.

Three weeks ago a local bank had received two hundred dollar bills from that heist. The FBI was immediately called in to investigate.

They quickly traced the bills to Attorney John Durham Smith who had rented the locker.

They visited his office to apprehend him when he opened fire at one of the FBI agents. A second agent returned fire and killed him.

Until now, they had never been able to locate the remaining dollars that had been stolen.

Even though I had purchased the remains of this locker, the robbery money in the Sterling Hotel safety deposit box belonged to the bank, and only the bank.

The bank offered me a reward. I refused and told them to give it to local charity in my name.

Albert and I collected our stash, but it didn't amount to the several hundreds of thousands of dollars that the bank had recovered.

My tractor, automobile tires, engagement ring and assorted broken jewelry netted me just over $11,000. Not bad for a $110 investment!

Albert unloaded his findings that were valued at $100. His investment had been only $5. The rest was junked. He was not disappointed, but thought my luck was worth the whole day. The lesson of this story is that you never know what a gamble can bring.

We all should know that life is truly a gamble in every sense of the word and that life "without a gamble" is no life at all.

Attorney Bernie's Married Life

*T*here is no connection to the popular jazz song *"My Attorney Bernie"* written by composer-pianist Dave Frishberg.

My Attorney Bernie graduated number three in his class at Harvard law School.

He went to work at the famous law firm of O'Brien, O'Brien and Goldberg in Boston.

Bernie passed the Bar in Boston (and every bar throughout the city).

He had become an alcoholic during high school and he was to carry that addiction well into his adult life.

He met a charming secretary, Norma Parente, at the firm. After a six-month affair they decided to get married.

Four months later they began fighting and drinking. Soon they legally divorced.

They had purchased a condo and Norma ended up retaining the mortgage and property. They split the bank account, each getting some $3,500 (funds mostly from their wedding).

Bernie kept the BMW and the loan to go with it.

The following year, he met and pursued Alice Hazburo, the daughter of a major toy manufacturer.

After a one-year relationship, they married. The marriage lasted three years. Their divorce created a legal mess.

They had built a townhouse in the suburbs valued at $375.000. Neither wanted the property. It went up for sale.

It was eventually sold for $310,000 -- a $65,000 loss. They both had to split the shortfall to repay the bank that was holding the mortgage.

Alice had her share. Bernie did not have the funds.

He was forced to take a loan from his firm.

Bernie met another sweetheart, Elizabeth Snooker, who made Bernie sign a marriage agreement that protected her fortune from him. All of it would go to her younger sister.

After the honeymoon, Elizabeth decided that Bernie didn't fill her needs and immediately applied for divorce. Bernie lost out once again.

Poor Bernie. Now at the age of seventy-three he was desperate for a companion in his old age.

He joined a singles matching program recommended on television.

Veronica Hubercarchi answered his ad. They dated for several weeks.

Veronica wanted to marry immediately. Bernie was fearful, but he decided to marry her anyway.

Yes, another mistake for Attorney Bernie.

He soon discovered that Veronica had been married and divorced five times, had seven children, and had spent three years in the Women's Reformatory in Framingham, Massachusetts for robbery. She quickly cleaned out $1,400 from his only savings account at the local bank.

She stole all of Bernie's assets from his apartment, which included several antique items that had been given to him from his mother.

He confronted her and demanded explanation. She answered, "My lawyer will be contacting you about our divorce... and giving me half of whatever you have left."

Bernie was to pay dearly for his choices in women and his inability to make any of his many relationships work.

In his depression, he wanted to contact Dr. Kevorkian from Minnesota, an expert in assisted suicide. He was about to make the call when he inadvertently slipped on a banana peel in his kitchen and fell to his death.

The Juicy Yellow Banana Company, of San Jose, Costa Rica, used parts of Attorney Bernie's slipping story as a joke in their promotions.

The moral of this story is: When legal troubles can't be resolved, slip on a banana peel and end it all.

Kicking the Bucket

The expression "Kicking the Bucket" appears to have been initially developed in England centuries ago. The expression has had a variety of use over the years

One of the earliest uses was at hangings when someone might kick the bucket under the hanging body, to "finish the job."

In American slang, it most often refers to a quick way to die.

Dr. Rick Wellsburg of Trumpsville, New Jersey developed a terrific game for the whole family, called "Kicking the Bucket, for Fun."

The game is sold in a kit. The kit contains six assorted buckets (all with handles). The buckets are made of galvanized metal, aluminum, wood, plastic, pottery and cardboard. It includes instructions on how to play the game.

The kits are currently available at CNT, K-Mart, Tooley's and Bon-ticy in South Africa.

Funeral Directors from all over the country are promoting these "Kicking the Bucket, for Fun" kits.

Dr. Rick's two offices are both located in Fall River, Massachusetts next to the Fall River International Airport. Dr. Rick is working on four more games for the whole family, soon to be released to the public.

His corporation is named Killer Games. Stock is available "over the counter" with the letters KGB at 40 cents per share.

The moral of this story is, when addressing your "bucket list," be careful what you KICK.

Al Capone's Favorite Murder

Although the Capone era is long gone, many new stories continue to surface.

I would like to attempt to create another scenario that might have fit into this long and terrible reign of corruption in Chicago. The characters and incidents are but the imagination of the author.

Otto Von Gramitt grew up in Bonn, West Germany. He attended Staad Military School.

He became a sharpshooter and learned to carry a small weapon to protect himself. His reputation quickly grew as being a rather tough character.

Otto established an early relationship with the Geutch-Borg Unit, which many years later became a part of Hitler's Nazi orgnization.

Among the many concerns of this organization was the advancement of several nearby countries that indicated that they might overthrow the existing German government, which at this time, was barely holding control.

This list of countries included Italy. Otto was asked to help keep the Italian people from their influence or action toward the German situation. He was sent to Rome and Florence to spy on several radical groups.

Otto learned quickly to dislike most of the groups. They talked and planned ways to remove the existing German top officials.

Anxious to make a name for himself among individuals in the German government, he reported the names and locations of some twenty-seven Italian radicals and assured the German Government that these radicals would not again be a problem for Germany.

He began eliminating them, one by one. Within two weeks he had killed all twenty-seven and escaped Italy.

The Italian Government put out a reward for his capture. They began to send operatives to Germany to search for him.

Top German officials recommended that Otto leave their country as soon as possible. They even gave him the funds to go.

He quickly took the next available aircraft and headed for America.

Otto landed in Chicago.

Soon he began working for a laundry that had a group of rentable washing machines and dryers. He was assigned to maintain and repair these machines.

Within a short time, he had learned a new profession. He decided to open up his own small laundry.

Two years later, he bought another small unit after the owner passed away. The widow sold it for pennies.

Otto's luck continued, and within four years he was the owner of six such units all in the city of Chicago.

He had become quite wealthy. He decided to spend his time going from unit to unit collecting cash. He was a happy immigrant.

But the timing was not great for Otto Von Gramitt. Gang warfare in the greater Chicago area had come to a peak.

A little known but tough racketeer named Al Capone had fought his way to the top in the Windy City by eliminating a number of fierce competitors. Many lives were lost during his rise to power.

Among his methods of collecting money was to threaten individuals, particularly prominent business people.

Capone's thugs approached Otto Von Gramitt at his successful enterprise. They wanted 10% of his gross each month.

Otto refused. When they threatened him, he returned the scare with his own threat.

His attitude was quickly reported directly to Capone.

Capone chose to visit Otto himself. "I'll cut you to threads if you don't meet our request," he said and quickly left the premises.

When he arrived back at his office, Capone was confronted by one of his assistants who had done a background check on Otto Von Gramitt.

Otto's past in Europe was now spelled out on paper. His killings in Italy had not been resolved by the Italian Government. They were still looking for him to face punishment for his brutal assassinations.

Al Capone smiled and exclaimed, "I'll do my best for my mother country. I'll remove him... and I'll collect the cash from his enterprise. I love cash in my pocket so I'll do it myself."

Otto never received another chance. Capone went into his personal office and shot him five times.

He had his thugs pick-up the body and had it delivered to his friend Tony the Butcher.

Tony was asked to sever the body into four parts. Each piece was to be boxed, with a letter written in German, and sent directly to Otto's proud organization, the Geutch-Borg Unit which by now had become part of Hitler's Nazi Party in Berlin.

The letter identified that the pieces were the remains of their trusty agent who had finally paid his dues to the Italian Government.

This was Al Capone's favorite murder.

Sir Winston Churchill Wants to Return

One of world's greatest statesmen, Sir Winston Churchill, applied to God for the opportunity to return to his precious England.

He had served his country and the world during difficult times in the 20th Century. He was truly one

of the world's most important men during that crucial period.

Although he passed away in 1965, he longed to come back to finish a little business.

Finally, after fifty years since he left our Earth, he received his permission from God to return, but with conditions. God make it clear that he could not criticize anyone who has served Great Britain since his passing or dispute any changes that might have taken place.

Sir Winston looked good when he arrived for the short visit. He had put on a few pounds and showed his advancement in age.

But, Winston was still Winston. He walked his usual stroll with a small cane in his right hand. His famous smile radiated and he spoke in his special way.

"I have come before you to remind the world that peace among us must be at all times our goal, without pause and without bias.

"We owe this generation and future generations the continued pursuit to that end.

"If I had been given an extension in life, I would have dedicated my existence toward that pursuit.

"Now I must return to the place from whence I came.

"But before I go, I've been allowed to take a handful of items with me.

"You would have probably guessed, a large bottle of sherry-wine and a box of my favorite cigars.

"God bless the Queen of England.

"And P.S. it was the late comedian George Burns who had last acted as God in the Hollywood movies, who had arranged this special trip for me.

"I am thankful to God and Mr. Burns for this opportunity."

No Clams in the Chowder

Clams from the ocean cost a lot of money these days.

The labor to get them from the ocean, the handling, and the transportation, all lead to an increase in price like many products today.

More people are eating them due to diets and other health issues. The increase in the population worldwide has an added effect on their demand.

And it costs more than five-clams to buy a bowl of decent chowder these days.

Recently, John Jackson of Malibu Beach, California developed a New England clam chowder -- without clams in it.

John claims he runs clams through the soup four times before completing the batch for public consumption.

His chowder brings $7 a bowl at both of his upscale John's Irregular Seafood Villas in the nearby Hollywood area.

By twelve noon at both addresses, the locals are waiting in line. The flavor of his chowder is terrific, with plenty of stock, mostly soft- potatoes and hints of celery and carrots. A second bowl is half-price.

Orders to go are a regular occurrence.

What an American success story this has become.

But where is this country heading if you can't even get clams in your clam chowder?

At this rate we probably won't get ice-cream in our hot-fudge sundae.

Daffy Duck Wows the Kentucky Derby

Not many ducks attend the Kentucky Derby.

The maintenance crew prepares the entire area around the racetrack for this special event weeks before the actual date.

The trained crew had already inspected all the possible crevices and overhangs that animals or other creatures might use to get free admission to this prize event.

Daffy Duck knew this happens every year. His plans were to work around their inspections. He had it all figured out.

Daffy grew up in Saratoga Springs, New York. His mother was a regular visitor to the race track there. His sister, Lolita sold "green-sheets" -- a horse handicapper's bible which is available at most race tracks.

She was known for her colorful smile and quick delivery. The IRS had been trying to catch up with her for nearly ten years. Her tips alone could support most of the animal kingdom. She never paid taxes of any kind.

Daffy told his family that he was destined to become involved in bigger and better things.

He left Saratoga Springs for the Mecca of horse racing: Lexington, Kentucky and the famous Kentucky Derby.

When he arrived, he set up his headquarters on the rooftop of an abandoned gas station. It still had Shell Oil Company signs all over the place.

The rooftop had a beautiful view of the distant race track. The location appeared to be super. No one would likely bother him here.

He spent the next two days checking the track and considering his many options. The plans for the big event were beginning to come together.

And then the day of the annual event finally arrived.

It was a bright Saturday with temperatures well into the 80's. There was no sign of rain. The wind was very soft and the air was hardly moving.

The crowd began arriving. The parking areas were quickly filling up. Security people seemed to be everywhere.

The Kentucky State Police were at each corner leading up to the entrance gates.

Individuals were beeping horns and music seemed to come from autos and speakers all around.

High fashions were seen coming out of cars, vans and busses, with people walking and talking along the pathways that stretched to the gates.

Many ladies were dressed in long gowns with distinctive colorful hats, and most had wide brims and were adorned with decorative arrangements.

The gents were also well dressed in stylish suits and jackets. Many wore hats, some straw and others appeared to be leather. They too captured the uniqueness of the event.

From a duck's standpoint this setting was indeed very impressive. Not many ducks had ever seen a vision like this up close. Daffy felt quite lucky.

He had done his homework and was poised to meet his planned objective. It was his time to fly to the roof of the paddock where he could observe each horse and jockey as they cleared the important weigh-in.

Colorful uniforms graced each individual number, from one to twelve.

Number one was "Clairmont," a 30-to 1 dark horse in red. Number two was "Leave-it-to-Frank," the 5-to 4 favorite in emerald-green. Number three "Fertil-Iza" who had been "scratched" due to a weight problem and a disturbing smell, had been dressed in powder blue.

Number four was "Sam's Short Pants," a 10-to-1 possible leader in bold-black. Number five was "Fried Bananas," listed at 9-to-1 in banana yellow. Number six, in dark battleship gray, was "Buckle

Your Headgear," a previous Derby Winner shown at 7-to-1 and was also considered to be a dark horse.

Number seven was "Seven-Eleven-Forever," an even money, last-minute entry, in beautiful pink. This horse had qualified just yesterday.

Number eight was named "Mom's Social Security," a 20-to-1 entry in dark-brown. Number nine was "Wicked Waltham," in washable-white, whose jockey had gotten sick and was forced to scratch.

Number ten was "Mustard and Relish," a possible favorite at 5-to-l, in faded-mustard yellow. Number eleven was "Four Dollar Gas," a 7-to-l entry in fancy tan.

And number twelve was "My Mother-In-Law's Money," an excellent "mudder" at 7-to-l, in purple silk.

Daffy noted each one, the way they looked, the way they strode, and the physical condition that they appeared to be in.

Sitting at the top of the clubhouse were several large crows. They appeared to have a bag of money.

Daffy thought that if he could give them information, he would not only make some friends, but maybe they would award him a well-deserved commission.

It looked like a no-brainer. He opened his wings and flew gently to the clubhouse roof top just ahead.

"Number eight, Mom's Social Security, looks the best. She seems to have the stride, quickness and mental seriousness to win this derby," Daffy contributed. "And, her jockey is a big winner up here, if that means anything."

"I'm Daffy Duck from New York. Who are you guys?"

"I'm Chrumpy and he's Craftie Crow from Cranston, Rhode Island," the largest Crow responded. "And these are our children, Christian and Cruser. We came here for the event."

"If there's money in that bag you are holding, I recommend putting most of it on "Mom's Social Security" wearing number eight," Daffy blurted.

Chrumpy Crow quickly responded. "Thank you for the info... but they won't take my money at the windows. However, I spotted Sonny the Squirrel down below and he has been known to take a bet or two. And so, I will be chasing him in a few minutes to attempt a reasonable bet."

Sure enough the Squirrel showed his shadow down below and Chrumpy jumped on him to place his "reasonable bet."

The Crows invited Daffy to stay with them during the race and he graciously accepted the kind offer.

The big race was about to begin. The place had been stuffed to the limit, as usual. The media was everywhere. A Who's Who of celebrities was in attendance and the weather was terrific.

The horses were getting ready at the gate. The number four horse was jumpy and the jockey fought to control the animal.

The gun fired a few seconds later, and they were off and running.

Mustard and Relish took the lead, followed closely by Leave-it-to-Frank.

Around the first turn, it was still Mustard and Relish but Mom's Social Security had taken over second place. Seven-Eleven-Forever was coming up on the outside, followed by Fried Bananas.

At the halfway point, it was still Mustard and Relish with Fried Bananas saddled in second place. Mother's Social Security was making a move on the inside.

Taking the final turn, it was Mother's Social Security trailing Mustard and Relish by a spoonful. It was beginning to look like a great finish ahead.

Mustard and Relish was barely holding on to its lead when Mother's Social Security picked up steam to win at the finish line by a nose.

The photo finish confirmed Mother's Social Security as the winner.

Mustard and Relish came in second and Seven-Eleven-Forever took third.

Mother's Social Security paid a handsome $37 and a two-dollar ticket won $74.

The runner-up, Mustard and Relish, paid $11 and the show ticket yielded $6.

Chrumpy Crow and his family had bet their fortune on the winner. The Squirrel was to pay them some five thousand-forty-six dollars!

But where was the Squirrel? His shadow could not be found.

Daffy decided to help in the chase. He flew around the clubhouse and paddock looking for his big tail.

Finally, he spotted him under the Paddock's watering hole, in the front of stall number seven.

And there he was holding on to the bag of money. "The Crows are looking for you. They expect full payment right now!" Daffy shouted.

"I will make good. You can assure them," the squirrel responded.

"Hop on," he insisted. "I'll take you right to them now. Don't put it off."

The Squirrel jumped on Daffy Duck's back and they flew to the roof top and the awaiting Crows.

"Nice going Daffy. You deserve a reward. But according to my math Sonny, you owe us well over five thousand dollars!" Chrumpy Crow shouted. "Just give us five thousand and keep the rest."

The Squirrel paid the five thousand and left in a hurry.

The Crows offered $500 to Daffy but he refused stating, "You guys bet your fortune and deserve every nickel. It was my pleasure to have helped you. You'll do something good for someone else in the future. I'm glad you got your reward for believing in me."

Word got out to the local press who put the story on the front page of their current edition. Other media people began using the story throughout the country and beyond.

Daffy Duck became an international hero. His story took away from the race winner "Mom's Social Security" but the horse's payoff of millions of dollars was still the biggest sport's news at the Derby.

The *New York Times* Editor questioned the story but finally agreed that it was just "ducky." Others thought he shouldn't have accepted it. Even the sportswriter for the *Times* called him a "Quack."

A Sardine Sandwich
for Amelia Earhart

My name is Nancy Flairfield.

I packed the final lunch for Amelia Earhart.

She wanted a soft sardine sandwich with ketchup and pickles spread throughout. This was her favorite meal while flying.

Amelia Mary Earhart was an American aviator and author who was the first female aviator to fly solo across the Atlantic Ocean.

She attempted to fly around the world in July 1937.

With the poor communications of the day she became lost early in the flight.

After she disappeared, I was approached by much of the local, national and international media to tell what I knew about her planned trip.

My sardine sandwich became very popular -- I was making them seven days a week for some thirteen years after her voyage began.

They named a street after me in my hometown and the sandwich made it to culinary institutions around the globe. Of course, Amelia was never found and foreign searchers used trained sensitive sniffing police dogs to attempt to locate the sardine smell from my sandwich all along her known flying route.

It was obviously to no avail.

The price for sardine packets rose from ninety cents to a dollar twelve during that time when my sandwiches were popular.

Some people think that this is a fishy story. I counter that if it "smells like sardines---it probably came from my kitchen."

I guarantee my customers that my sardines are always fresh, and when I place them on a sandwich, they are hardly moving.

Ella Fitzgerald's Return to Music

Ella left this planet some years ago. No one has risen to replace her. Many have tried and some are actually darn good. But critics agree that there probably won't be another Ella.

Therefore, the author, being a jazz critic, has decided so to speak, to bring her back to this Earth. "*That's why the Lady is a Tramp*."

Ella arrived via Trump Airlines at the Fall River International Airport in Massachusetts. Duke Ellington sent a limo to pick her up.

The driver took her to Boston's Symphony Hall for a command performance with the Duke Ellington Orchestra.

It had been sold-out weeks in advance. Tickets were going for $200 apiece.

A local radio station auctioned-off a pair of tickets for charity at $3,000 each.

The Ellington Orchestra was to have Dizzy Gillespie and Miles Davis up front with Stan Getz filling in on reeds. Ella was to be truly in "Heaven."

John and Jackie Kennedy, and Tip O'Neil, had the best seats in the house. Governor John Volpe and his wife had the adjacent table. Barney Frank and his friend shared the next prize seats.

Sports legends Red Auerbach, Ted Williams and Bobby Orr were seen at another table.

People arrived in fancy clothes making the event even more special. Women were wearing colorful gowns and gentlemen were clothed in fashionable suits and jackets.

Massachusetts Avenue in Boston's Back Bay was backed-up with traffic like never before.

Ella was about to perform. She was ready.

Boston's famous maestro, Arthur Fiedler, was acting as master of ceremony. The hall quieted to a whisper. You could hear a pin drop.

The Duke Ellington Orchestra was introduced.

They began with their nostalgia numbers that brought them fame. Four upbeat tunes in a row thrilled the audience.

Arthur Fiedler returned to the stage. He defined the historic background of the featured gifted songstress who was about to perform for the audience.

Ella glided across the orchestra's front. She was dressed in a magnificent rose and white low-cut chemise floral gown created by Oscar de la Renta. Her well-known smile graced her coiffed propped African- American hairdo with accents of sparkling red. The glitter made her stand out against the great orchestra behind her. When the applause lowered, she broke into "Embraceable You" (written by the late George Gershwin). Her rendition was already worth the price of admission.

She stroked with passion and vibrato of the melody, slowing at each precious stop, with her own perfect pitch to the delight of the audience.

Her second number was "A Tisket-a-Taskit," followed by the theme song "Emily" from the Hollywood motion picture "The Americanization of Emily" that starred Julie Andrews.

Her fourth and final composition for the first phase of the program was "Mack-The-Knife." The audience went wild with this special number. They began dancing in the aisles.

When she finished, the whole place stood and applauded her and the great Ellington Orchestra.

Ella had returned.

Miles Davis and Dizzy Gillespie with horns, and Stan Getz, with his reeds, came out on stage next.

They quickly began "When the Saints Go Marching In."

A surprised guest walked out to participate. It was the great trombonist Al Grey. He immediately picked-up on "The Saints" and soon performed a solo-take to contribute.

Ella returned to the stage and this sensational group slowed down to bring her voice into the next elongated, repeated stanza.

It was truly a gas.

The Ellington Orchestra returned to perform. Their Sammy Mestaco arrangement of "Autumn in New York" allowed Ella to do a magnificent rendition of this beautiful standard.

Woohs and ahhhs were heard throughout the hall.

"My Funny Valentine" followed. It was a tear-jerker. There were many wet eyes. Ella was truly at her best.

Miles, Dizzy, Stan and Al Grey filled in for three more numbers.

Ella finished with two final solo ballads. They were "Never Let Me Go" and "Days of Wine & Roses."

The full orchestra, along with Ella singing and performing "Wonderful World," ended the program.

Jazz had never received such a reprise. Only God could have arranged this happening.

The author had put together this retake of music's spectacular past. No doubt jazz enthusiasts might have spent the $200 for such a ticket.

Long live the everlasting memory of those departed jazz greats and their spectacular skills.

The Lovable Fat Henry

Clarence "Fat" Henry was born at 27 pounds. By the time he was two years old his weight was already 55 pounds.

When he entered pre-school, he was wearing young men's clothing and was weighing nearly 80 pounds. The other kids at pre-school loved him. He was jolly and playful and did everything he could to make friends.

Henry arrived at first grade weighing 110 pounds. He stood nearly five feet tall. His effervescent smile and loveable grace won him instant friendships. He was the talk of the school.

He was to finish high school weighing over 290 pounds and standing six-feet six inches tall. His width was 48 inches and he needed most of two seats to sit comfortably.

Fat Henry's mother and father were normal in size and were overwhelmed by their son's growth.

Their son's personality and warmth overshadowed his physical appearance. He was so loveable that everyone that knew him truly appreciated the gift of his unusual personality.

In his junior year of high school, he was so popular that he was voted class president. He did such a great job they re-elected him to lead in his senior year, too. He was also named "The Most Likely to Succeed."

To top it off, he became the valedictorian and was named the keynote speaker at graduation.

He delivered a spectacular speech reminding his fellow students that "just because others are not physically normal doesn't mean that they are less human or have less intelligence. Furthermore, the world need not address them any differently than any other human being."

Everyone stood and applauded. All of his fellow students, teachers, family and friends remained on their feet for several minutes acknowledging his dynamic speech.

"Fat-Henry" was then presented with the annual Community Excellence Award, and with it came a four-year scholarship to Piedmont University.

Four years later, after graduating number three in his college class of nine hundred, he opted to become a professional speaker.

He spoke regularly to local organizations, school gatherings, military groups, corporate meetings and government seminars.

His speeches would highlight the physically different. He would regularly point out that many obese individuals were born with thyroid deficiency, and others are born with symptoms that turn into catalysts that promote many irregular physical developments.

"Fat-Henry" joined several national and international organizations formed for the physically-handicapped. He became a spokesperson for them throughout his career. He encouraged individuals to join these organizations and participate in their objectives and growth.

"Fat-Henry" won the hearts of many Americans. Although he was oversized and overweight, he never let these irregularities stop him from fitting into normal situations, always encouraging acceptance on an equal basis.

He attempted to join the military but was declined because of his size. "Fat-Henry" decided that there were other ways to serve our nation. He volunteered as a speaker during basic-training activities at several important military locations. He received no pay for his effort.

The President of the United States even gave him special honors at a White House dinner.

His example won him the Man of the Decade Award in Detour Magazine.

"Fat Henry" stories continue to this day.

The moral of this story is that there is always a way to help offset one's irregularities, achieve self-esteem and enjoy a wonderful life.

Long live "Fat-Henry."

Congress Cuts Half
of Annual Foreign Aid

Washington, D.C.

The Congress of the United States has announced the passage of a major bill, proclaiming that one-half of all foreign aid has been deleted from the annual federal budget.

The White House has scheduled a news conference for 1:00 p.m. to report to the nation how this "windfall" is expected to be applied.

The President and several leaders of Congress will be facing the media in this rare bipartisan address.

According to the President's speech (advance copies have just released from the White House) the following will be included in his formal statements at the conference:

1. We will use part of the savings to eliminate poverty in this country.

2. We will use part of the savings to eliminate homelessness in this country.

3. We will use part of the savings to guarantee that our veterans receive everything that they have earned and deserve.

4. We will use part of the savings to secure our borders which have been penetrable for too long.

5. We will use part of the savings to fix our roads, infrastructure, bridges, buildings, airports and train stations.

6. We will use part of the savings to reboot our education system at all levels.

7. We will use part of the savings to forgive ninety percent of college loans across the nation.

8. We will use part of the savings to give two years of free education at public junior colleges to high school graduates.

9. We will use part of the savings to give each middle-class American a special $1000 tax bonus, immediately.

10. We will use part of the savings to reduce each household annual income tax bill by $1000.

11. We will use part of the savings to reward industry for new products, ideas and for the creation of new jobs.

12. We will use part of the savings to offer everyone, who needs it, free healthcare.

13. We will use part of the savings to give our senior citizens a twenty percent raise in Social Security.

14. We will use part of the savings to begin to eliminate our federal debt which should be repaid within a couple of years.

15. We will use part of the savings to revise our election system to modern times, where the people's vote, and only the people's vote, elect our political leaders.

Bang! Bang! Bang!

The author has awakened; he had been dreaming.

What a shame. It is unfair to think that this has been only a dream.

Maybe this story will awaken the leaders of our country who definitely require waking.

Ten Dollars per Gallon for Gas

The price of gasoline at the pumps differs around the globe.

The Unites States has enjoyed the luxury of reasonable rates up until a few decades ago.

Before that, prices started at around a dollar. It began to climb from there to around two dollars per gallon.

In the middle of this decade, the gallon rose to nearly four dollars in many sections of our country.

Today it seems to bounce back and forth between two dollars to nearly three dollars per gallon.

Oil from the Far East and other locations determines the base price per barrel. Transportation and processing labor costs tends to produce the daily delivered price to the petrol stations. When a glut in the market occurs, the price usually drops in our favor.

Then the petrol station adds a chosen profit to the daily delivered price and that is what they advertise on their signs attracting us, as buying customers.

Norbit Clayborn, a petrol station owner in Newark, New Jersey, decided to sell his regular gas (78 octane) at ten dollars per gallon. His high-test (91 octane) is sold at thirteen dollars per gallon.

Norbit says, "I'm in a busy market place with continual traffic, pretty much twenty-four hours per day. I pay heavy taxes to be in this spot. My overhead for employees is quite high.

"I decided to charge this staggering price to attract a special group of drivers. Many don't care what the price is and their company's expense account absorbs the fee, without fanfare.

"A lot of old-timers and women don't follow gas prices and are always looking for the easiest situation. We sure make it as easy as possible. Our lanes are much wider for easy access. Our employees always do the pumping. We even offer to clean their windshield.

"Our employees are dressed in a shirt and bow tie, are properly attired and are clean looking. Courtesy is stressed in client relations.

"Most of our customers are repeat clients. Yes, we get new ones continually throughout the day, as well.

"There is no diesel gas or propane and no auto repairs or accessories are offered. We do not sell food; we just sell petrol.

"The finest of public restrooms are meticulously maintained.

"We don't advertise major brands. We just buy the cheapest fuel that is available. I'm well on my way to becoming a multi-millionaire."

The New Jersey Department of Commerce awarded Norbit The 2012 Success Story of the Year Award.

This story is a gas (but you don't have to leave the room for this one).

"My advice to you guys. Find yourself a spot and join in on the riches."

Peanuts for General Grant

U lysses S. Grant rose in the ranks to become general of the Union Army during the Civil War. Later, in 1869, he became the 18th President of The United States.

He had served his country, its military leaders and the Congress directly.

General Grant had also developed a liking for roasted peanuts.

Since his earliest days at West Point Military Academy, he regularly chomped on a variety of local peanuts.

When he became a ranking officer he appointed a military liaison to obtain and make peanuts available to him directly.

It was well known that at the Battle of Richmond, he was eating his favorite nuts while directing his troops in combat.

Later, when meeting with President Lincoln, he was observed offering some roasted almonds to the

President while briefing him on up-to-date war conditions.

The President replied, "if you keep chomping on nuts how will we win the war?"

Grant quickly replied, "it takes brains and an active mouth to conceive and communicate the proper commands that will enable our troops to win battles, Mr. President. Peanuts help my brains and my mouth accomplish those goals."

With that remark, President Lincoln asked for another handful. The meeting was completed.

Many Civil War historians believe that Virginia peanuts helped win the war for the Union Army. Others say, that only a nut would believe that statement.

But still others believe that since peanuts are a product of the South, that maybe the "Rebs" should have won the war.

Finding "Gold" in Newport, Rhode Island

Alfred (Fred) Byron-Swartz, very early in life, dreamed about finding gold.

When he was growing up in nearby Warwick, Rhode Island, he would envision making such a discovery. That vision would one day change his life.

"Maybe it could help me find the right lady to spend the rest of my days with? Maybe it could provide me with the financial security so that I'd never have to work for a living? Maybe it would assure me the good health necessary to live a long and happy life?"

But he knew that the gold discovery must happen first.

So Fred set out to find it.

He spent a day at the Newport Library researching the possibility. The library people told him that pirates were believed to have buried their booty (mostly stolen property) at hidden spots on the island.

There was a pamphlet that claimed a treasure map was hidden somewhere near the Middletown-Newport Beach line.

Fred decided to investigate the suspicion. He drove to this area and began searching in the water at low tide.

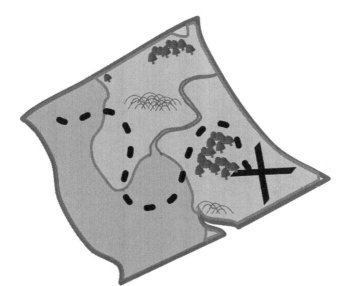

He noticed a broken rod protruding from the seawater about 100 yards out from the beach. He thought this rod might play a role in his search.

Reaching down around the rod he found a cloth bag that had been somehow attached to the broken rod.

In retrieving the cloth bag, he noticed it was more than half eaten away, probably eroded by the tides over a long period of time.

He gently handled the bag and observed a parchment of some sort within its ragged cover.

Wisely, he set the discovery down to dry out. The strong sun of the day quickly began to dry the heavily watered bag.

A short time later, he was able to take an old and smeared parchment from within the tattered bag.

The parchment was indeed a map of some sort. The map was blurred but showed distinctive lines that might indicate direction. He realized this was probably the map that the library pamphlet had mentioned.

Fred interpreted the directions on the parchment and quickly discovered the metal box that had been hidden about 200 feet from the broken rod.

Upon opening the box, which had been embellished with tiny mussels attached to it, he found an array of booty.

Within were several odd bars of gold, gold jewelry, a gold pot and pieces of gold fragments piled against the walls.

The box was heavy, indicating that the gold was real.

"It must be worth millions!" he exclaimed. "I have hit the pirates' treasure and I will be rich!"

Suddenly, a loud blast occurred.

Fred woke up to find he had been dreaming.

He had been asleep in the front seat of his trusty old convertible, parked along the side the Greenvale Winery in Portsmouth, Rhode Island on a Saturday afternoon where a weekly jazz performance was about to be started.

"Wow! I thought I was rich and now I realize that it was only a dream," he said to himself softly.

"I'm just a retired old goat with little money to live on, and lousy health to boot. Best I go in and have Dick play 'Green Dolphin Street' for me."

He hobbled his way into the wine-tasting building. It was packed with jazz enthusiasts and large groups of young people.

There were no empty chairs. He shouted loudly, "find me a chair, please! And I have brought my lunch and need some wine. Or must I pay for it... like most people here."

Rick Wells gave him a rousing drum roll. Wow.

Christiana found him a broken chair and he placed it against the door, almost kissing the band.

Rena brought him a wine glass and proceeded to take his twenty-dollar bill. She placed the bill up toward the light to make sure the currency was real. Everyone who was watching his grand entrance began to laugh.

It was truly a sight to behold. The entertainment provided by Fred was nearly as good as that of the jazz combo.

Jennifer Wells took some pictures and Nancy Parenti waved to him.

Fred was now settled down in the midst of all the activity. How lucky he was to arrive late (as usual) and to enjoy the comfort of the people around him.

Alfred (Fred) Byron realized that even though he had lost his dream of gold, he had found by luck, a warm and important spot here where he could listen to live jazz -- an art form that he had savored for most of his long life.

The moral of this story is that gold may have its advantages, but it does not necessarily replace much of what is truly valuable in life, and incidentally, often happens to be free.

Greenberg the Priest

*A*lthough this story is not true, I believe that it could actually have happened under long and difficult wartime circumstances.

I served six years in the U.S. Army myself and later became an historian of the Second World War. Several of my relatives and friends served in this conflict. I grew up during the actual war period.

I have written many books, including "'Round Newport," based upon some sixty years of attendance at the Newport Jazz Festival, in Newport, Rhode Island.

The mighty 189th U.S. Army Infantry Battalion came off a destroyer onto the beach at Iwo Jima, a Japanese occupied island in the South Pacific during World War II. It was important for the U.S. Army to capture this island linking it to the ongoing pathway to Japan, where they were anxious to repay the Japanese for the humiliating destruction of our military at Pearl Harbor in Hawaii.

The men of the 189th had been training in advanced infantry warfare of the day. They had helped round up Japanese citizens and agents in Hawaii after the Pearl Harbor disaster, but they had never been in the jungle or had experienced the fierce fighting that they were about to encounter.

Colonel Rick Wells, a graduate of West Point, was the commanding officer. The thirty-two-year-old had served in China for two years at the American Embassy. He was married and had three children.

The executive officer was Second-Lieutenant Harry O'Brien, a UCLA graduate with an ROTC background. He was twenty-four years-old and never had military training. He had been assigned to the 189th just two weeks earlier.

Harry had become the joke of the unit. He didn't even know how to pack a field bag. What use would he be to this group? Only time would tell.

Sgt. Major Paul Helmbrecht had participated in the end of World War I. He had spent twenty-seven years in the Army and now at forty-nine years-old, was to be the veteran of this put together battalion.

He had been elected to train this group, organize their schedules, develop their courage and determination, and warn them of what could be facing them in future engagements.

Sgt. Paul wasn't sure of their actual abilities in face to face combat. He told the commander and his staff about his concerns. Even division headquarters became aware of it.

Yet these had become "emergency times" and our military had been spread throughout the world. Unknown situations had to be tested everywhere.

The unit consisted of ninety-one men, and only six were officers.

Roger Anderson had but two hours of medical film training. He was a private first class, one of the lowest ranks in the service. He was considered the "doctor" of the unit.

Billy Gramitt had been trained on the BAR automatic machine gun. Billy had come from New Britain, Connecticut and was eighteen years-old.

Billy dropped out of high school when America came into the War. The Army had wisely kept him away from Germany, as his ancestors were German born.

Billy was a wise-guy, very outspoken and a potential troublemaker.

Peter Gates had been released from the seminary for outspoken behavior. The Army quickly promoted him to company priest, the unit's holy man, who would be expected to help maintain courage and resolve for any of the soldiers that needed it. He carried a bible next to his heart, but couldn't believe the Army's expectations for him.

Bobby Linzer, Norman Renzi and Alfonzo King were the sharpshooters of the unit. They had scored highest at the various training ranges and were awarded medals for their skills.

Nineteen-year-old Barney Greenberg had been released from a bad-boys school in upstate New York. He had been there for three years because he had stolen a bicycle from his neighborhood. He had enlisted in the Army for two years. He had been trained at Fort Dix, New Jersey and just assigned to the 189th.

Sgt. Mark Van Earl was the supply chief and was active in food distribution. He was thirty-six years-old and was from Cleveland, Ohio. He had been serving in the Ohio National Guard when war broke out. He was now a key veteran in this group.

The remaining members of the 189th are not important to this story, although their effort in the service to our nation is well worth another story all on its own.

***

The troop carriers from the destroyer hit the water at five in the morning. They were quickly filled with the men of the 189th Battalion. They were headed to the shoreline of Iwo Jima.

Thirty-one U.S. Navy ships of all sizes had bombarded the harbor and the interior. There was no sign of enemy resistance.

It looked like the troop landing would be an easy success.

But Japanese soldiers were dug deep into beach fortifications. Those that had survived the Navy bombardment were still ready to greet the expected troop invasion.

Many were supplied with automatic weapons and they opened fire immediately when the oncoming troops came within range on the beachhead. It was going to be messy.

A large percentage of the first wave of soldiers never reached the sandy cliffs and beach entries. Casualties mounted quickly. Heavy fighting was exchanged.

Hand-grenades and flamethrowers picked apart the remaining Japanese that had occupied the beachhead.

Finally, the beat-up 189th made it to shore. But they had paid the price.

Colonel Rick Wells had taken some shrapnel and was bandaged on the right arm.

The company Priest Paul Gates had been shot in the back and was put on a stretcher. It was to become his ticket home for hospitalization somewhere in the states.

Norman Renzi, one of the three sharpshooters, had been killed before he hit the water. Thirteen others died in the invasion. Six others received injuries of which two were serious.

The unit had been reduced to seventy-one. The colonel still held onto his command.

***

Battalion Headquarters called the colonel to determine the number of men that remained able to fight.

He was told by headquarters, "leave the dead and the wounded behind and move slowly and surely

forward. A quartermaster's unit is right behind you. They will take care of the immovable."

And so the reduced 189th began their movement into the interior of the island.

A gun rattle took out two men. They found the culprit a few minutes later wedged into a tiny cave on the left side of the hill. Alfonzo King blasted away on his carbine. The sniper fell head-down in his hideout. They moved on.

Out in front was an area of palm trees and beyond that was a pond filled with water lilies.

High on the ridge overlooking the pond was a cement fortification. The colonel chose Sgt. Paul Helmbrecht and four others to circle around and take it out.

The sound of fierce fighting followed. Sgt. Paul and only one other returned.

The group moved into the pond area. The oppressive heat had played a toll on the entire unit. The colonel authorized everyone to get soaked. Shirts came off quickly, along with helmets and other gear. The colonel told them to make it quick.

Finally, after the quick wet-down, the group was split into two sections and was told to proceed around the mountain from the two sides until they met up. Strangely, there were no enemy encounters.

Billy Gramitt was having a tough time with dysentery. He was forced to give up his BAR weapon and return through the brush to the beach for help.

The gun was reassigned to the executive officer, Lieutenant Harry O'Brien.

They stopped to have chow. C-Rations were distributed to each of them. The food was far from excellent but when you are hungry, as they were, it tasted quite good.

While eating their rations they heard and observed a row of U.S. Army tanks breaking through terrain resistance off to the right. It indicated that other units were moving ahead as well.

Now the 189th moved forward. Ahead was open space -- dry and flat land. Scattered gun fire appeared to be coming from some piles of burned husks about one hundred feet ahead.

Lieutenant Harry O'Brien planted his BAR and sprayed the brush. Two Japanese soldiers jumped up with their hands in the air. Sgt. Paul raced forward and disarmed the willing prisoners.

The 189th reached the end of the open area and entered quickly into the tree-packed jungle.

It was then that Colonel Wells decided to stop for the evening. Darkness had begun to set in. It appeared that they had completed their first day on Iowa Jima.

The colonel appointed three men as guards, two in the front of the group, and one in the rear. Others were assigned relief duty throughout the night. Hopefully they could all get some rest.

The 189th had now been reduced to sixty-eight men. Colonel Wells had just gotten off the walkie-talkie and had received new orders for a movement at daybreak to a village approximately two miles away.

It was Sunday and a "Man of the Cloth" was needed for those men who wanted to pray.

Their priest, Pfc. Paul Gates, was shot in the back and had been sent back to the beachhead. Even though he had limited religious background, he had been assigned to be the unit chaplain.

Harry O'Brien appointed Pvt. Barney Greenberg to be the new priest. Greenberg had been born into an atheist family and knew very little about religion.

After a quick lecture by the lieutenant, Private Greenberg formed a group of about thirty men seeking a chance to pray on this dangerous morning. It was 3:30 a.m. The unit was to move out at 4.

Greenberg stood before the group and asked everyone to, "pray to your God." He asked them to "seek help to get through this battle and bring us safely home to our love ones in America."

He told everyone that he didn't like this job but would do the best he could.

From that time on they called him "Father Greenberg." He accepted the title and notoriety that came with it. He reacted, "I guess I've been called to serve."

***

Although the 189th eventually finished its objectives in the island fight, they shared their heroic achievements with many other military groups that also gave their finest to conquer the island.

It proved to be an important advancement toward our victory in the Pacific War.

The Japanese made gallant efforts to keep the island but were unable to stop the U.S. military whose persistent strength prevailed.

Father Barney Greenberg carried out his assignment throughout the Pacific campaign.

He was awarded several medals by the U.S. Army for his unusual service to our fighting men and to our nation.

Greenberg finished his four years in the service and became a popular speaker. His stories and wit attracted many organizations and gatherings around the country.

He married a devout Catholic, Mary C. McCoy, and began the study of many religions. Eventually he chose Judaism.

Barney Greenberg died on October 14, 1989, at the age of sixty-four after a battle with cancer. His four children proudly keep this unusual story alive. Their pride and appreciation of their father's service in the Pacific during World War II is Barney's greatest legacy.

The Reading of Herbie's Will

Herbert Carlton Hamberger had just turned 91 years old when he expired.

He had lived an interesting life, in-and-out of wealth, love, relationship with his family, and dealings with the government.

Herbie had also been fighting cancer for several years.

The family, business associates, friends and even some enemies were waiting with hope that Herbie would have remembered them financially in his last testament.

Herbie had destroyed his bridges with most everyone. He wanted to do things completely his way -- right to the end.

The tough old bird decided to surprise "all that would be waiting" in his custom-made personal will.

Only his lawyer, Maxwell Cohen, knew of his decisions.

It was a bright day in August when Attorney Maxwell Cohen called the group to order that had gathered into his client's plush office on the 32nd floor of the Alhambra Medical Building in downtown Fleece, North Dakota.

They had come from everywhere. The room was packed to its fullest. Many were standing in the back of the room. No extra chairs were to be found.

Herbie had made his fortune late in life. He had lost plenty in the stock market and in poor business dealings. Prior to his success, he'd had three wives.

Fifteen years ago he bought into the Ouch Medical Corporation, which specialized in inventing painless medical procedures. The company expanded and its concepts were adopted around the world.

Herbie's two-thousand-dollar investment had grown to about $10,000. Then he bought out two major investors and held their combined stock for the next three years.

The General Medical Corporation, Ltd. of England agreed to purchase the Ouch Medical Corporation at that time. His holdings were exchanged for two million dollars in the buyout.

Herbie immediately invested the money in several Wall Street favorites and it multiplied quickly.

He bought and sold regularly in the last few years of his life, building his estate to about twelve million dollars.

And now it was time for his Attorney Cohen to begin the reading of his will.

"I, Herbert C. Hamberger, of sound mind and conviction, on this 14th day of July, 2012, hereby instruct my trusted lawyer, Attorney Maxwell Cohen, to convey to these heretofore specific individuals my assets as instructed:

1. To my grandson Herbert Hamberger II: My 300 Playboy Magazines.

2. To my granddaughter Leigh-Leigh Hamberger: My four Andy Warhol paintings.

3. To my other granddaughter Porsha McGowen: My collection of Grandma Moses postcards.

4. To my son-in-law, Jason McGowen: My two letters from Vice President Spiro Agnew.

5.To my daughter-in-law Laurentine McGowen: The leather chair in my study.

6.To my so-called friend Barney Constantine: The used cigar Fidel Castro smoked during his visit to the UN Assembly.

7.To my first wife Mildred Aufhauser: My extra bottle of after-shave lotion labeled, "Never Again."

8.To my second wife Clarabella Seagrams: My last case of Canada Dry. (The bottles have returnable deposits for you.)

9.To my third wife Isadora Lipshitz: My final VISA credit card statement that she should pay without fanfare.

And finally...

10. To my daughter Elizabeth Hamberger: My Mercedes and one million dollars.

11. To my son William Hamberger: All my remaining stock, my real-estate holdings, and my precious wardrobe, plus one million dollars.

12. To my faithful servant Tommy Wang: $250,000. (And the scotch in the liquor-cabinet.)

13. To my trusted Lawyer, Attorney Maxwell Cohen, $500,000 (to finalize all legal costs to me, my family and estate).

14. To the Internal Revenue in Washington: My "Swampland" holdings in Florida and my shares in Bernie Madoff's investment scheme (and a copy of my final Federal Tax Return).

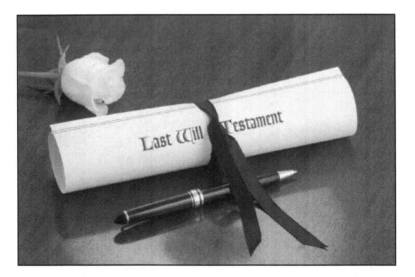

15. To my undertaker: Burn me to dust, and scatter what is left into the nearest pond. (And don't let my family make any changes to my wishes.)

"To those whom I neglected to award, I say 'sorry.' You obviously never meant enough to me to even consider leaving you anything. Too bad!

"The remaining millions of my earned assets are left to charity. I have given Attorney Cohen a list of twenty-three organizations that will share my final fortune.

"I believe that I will someday return, and you can bet that I will do things a lot differently.

"To the rest of you, just remember me as Herbie."

My Mother Stole Jelly Beans from President Ronald Reagan

President Ronald Reagan was known for his love of jelly beans.

Throughout his Hollywood days and his political ones, he probably digested many, many pounds of his favorite candy.

"Mr. Gorbachev take down that wall" were considered among his finest words. He will be forever remembered for that famous statement.

But to candy-store merchants, Reagan's love of jelly beans will always be the thing that first comes to mind.

I am Julie Cameron, of Chicago, Illinois. My mother Marie worked in the White House for some twelve years. She held the title of Room Superintendent.

It was her job to oversee each room after preparations were completed. She looked after each room in the White House.

I had the good fortune to have spent special time with my mother before her recent passing. She was able to tell me about many incidents that had occurred during her life, including several things that happened in the White House. She spoke of having to over-see the Oval Office almost every day.

The President's desk during the Reagan years was always covered with jelly beans and needed clearing so he could address his work of the day. The beans had to be gathered and put into a glass tumbler.

My mother, who claimed she loved jelly beans also, took advantage of the selection and helped herself to a few choice ones while doing her work.

One day the President walked in and caught her imbibing on a few of them and exclaimed, "caught you!" and began laughing about it.

He then continued, "I love the dark colored ones in particular, how about you?" In her embarrassment she replied, "I love the light colored ones myself."

"Good," he countered. "Then we have no problem. Help yourself."

From that moment on she enjoyed a few of Ronald Reagan's prize jelly beans almost daily.

My mother said that she had told that story to many of her friends and relatives and enjoyed the responses that came with it.

Yes, my mother stole jelly-beans from Ronald Reagan and now the world will know of it.

Lime Rickey to the Rescue

To a glass of club-soda, add a piece of lime and some sugar and you will have a refreshing drink for those hot summer days.

The drink is called a Lime Rickey.

Its popularity goes back to the mid-20th Century. There are now signs of its renewed popularity.

Major beverage manufacturers have been flirting with the recipes for several years.

Professor "Lime-Rickey" Wells, of Portsmouth, Rhode Island, had a serious hobby as a jazz drummer.

He had tired of his hobby, when his charming wife Jennifer encouraged him to produce a great Lime Rickey drink that could be sold to the public.

As a "cymbal" of his love for Jennifer, he decided to build a portable stand and "drum" up a successful business.

His Rickey drinks were put into appropriate envelopes, with plastic inner walls and kept in a large cooler.

The Professor put his stand on the Portsmouth end of The Mount Hope Bridge that connected Bristol, Rhode Island, to Aquidneck Island.

There, he would regularly "snare" a few customers each hour. He sold the drinks for nine cents each.

Eventually he used the funds to buy the bridge from the State of Rhode Island.

Jennifer painted the bridge pink in honor of "Pinky Lee," a favorite comedian from her youth.

She wanted to operate the toll booth where she would collect hub caps as the regular auto fee to drive the length of the bridge.

Professor Wells told us that the collection of hub caps would be used in a new family game that he had invented, that was to be released next year.

The moral of this story is that, "a good summer drink can always help you drum-up a successful adventure."

"But don't tell your mother."

Marilyn's Secret Lovers

The late controversial movie actress Marilyn Monroe (Norma Jeane Mortenson) was known not only for her beauty and acting skills, but also for her seductive adventures.

Although she passed away in August 1962, at age 36, she had experienced three marriages and many alleged affairs.

Two of her marriages were to famous men.

Her marriage to playwright Arthur Miller lasted just two years, and her marriage to baseball Hall of Famer Joe DiMaggio of the New York Yankees lasted less than a year.

She would party with John and Bobby Kennedy, Peter Lawford, Frank Sinatra and several Hollywood producers among others.

The tabloids didn't know about two other affairs that occurred and happened to be very special to Marilyn.

The first involved her milkman, Oliver Peacock, who was married with nine children.

Oliver visited her apartment every third day, leaving a quart of milk and enjoying an extra hour with her.

She really loved Oliver. Because he was married, she felt quite relaxed with him. And of course, he became very fond of her.

Their special happenings lasted about three years.

But when the cows that supplied the milk stopped producing, Oliver lost his job.

Soon Marilyn found another playmate. His name was Sergio Von Beckinberg, a race car driver from Austria.

She met him at the post office. They were both licking stamps. He blushed. She blushed. She made a comment. "My stamps taste lousy, how about yours?"

He introduced himself, and that was the beginning of a six-year romance that no one knew about.

They would meet at his garage in Malibu, each Wednesday evening. Above the garage was his apartment.

The apartment proved to be convenient for many of his other business transactions. The Internal Revenue Service eventually closed him down for cheating the U.S. government.

Marilyn went to court trying to help his case, but it was to no avail.

Sergio went to jail for ten years and was fined nearly a million dollars. He became penniless.

The moral of this story is that when you run out of milk and the Internal Revenue Service wants you, it is time to call it a day.

Marilyn tried a lot of different approaches for the love that she craved. When she passed away, we lost a special and unique entertainer.

Treasures on Nantucket Island

Carol Fence invited Nancy and me, and our friend Pat Queen, to enjoy an extended Labor Day weekend on Nantucket Island in Massachusetts.

Carol had purchased land on this special island many years ago. Then she built a lovely home on the property.

She furnished it in hand-picked contemporary marine motif. It became a wonderful laid-back retreat with all the fixings.

Nantucket is a fairly large island off the coast of Massachusetts that sits in the northern Atlantic Ocean pretty much by itself.

It takes a long ride on a ferry shuttle, or a rather expensive airplane ride from either Boston or Providence, to get there.

Nantucket is a model New England summer retreat with a variety of architecture.

The village (or city center) boasts streets lined with craft stores, eateries and a few national retail establishments. Seafood is featured across the island; it is fresh and darn good.

The city's patriotism and color seems to be everywhere. Locals attempt to sell their wares throughout the community. People are friendly and helpful. Just ask.

Carol's year-around home is in Jamestown, Rhode Island, just across the bay from the resort vacation attraction of Newport, Rhode Island.

There, she and Pat Queen enjoy oceanside condos nearly next to each other.

Carol drove us around Nantucket in her trusty jeep. And I became overwhelmed by our visit to the city dump. It became quite an adventure.

Cars lined the street entering the location. Carol had warned us it would be unusual.

There were people all around seeking entertainment and bargains. Obviously the massive collections were discards from the local inhabitants. But wow, it was a bonanza.

There were the usual clothes, books, magazines, toys and electrical throwaways. After a quick investigation, it appeared that most of the stuff was in perfect condition. It included games, furniture, relics and assorted accessories.

Visitors freely took whatever they wanted. They were coming and going at a regular rate.

Although it was tough, we finally found a decent parking space. It was now our turn.

I found a book on mesquite lava that sounded a bit interesting. Pat picked up a clay pot that had "Nantucket" written on it. Nancy found a fashion magazine written in Portuguese. Carol just stood there laughing.

Next, I wandered into the inner rooms and the rest of our group followed me.

I came across a small banged-up trumpet. Upon quick examination I believed that most of the bumps could be bent out of the instrument and would be fun to play with.

Carol lifted a picture of Richard Nixon that she thought could hang near the toilet at her summer cottage.

Nancy discovered a Ralph Lauren pocketbook with sparkling diamonds. Pat also found one in beautiful untouched leather, with a broken button-snap. She thought that she could easily replace the broken piece.

A truck backed into the entrance of an outer shed. It was loaded with new items.

We ran to the edge of the big truck. We were among the first to get there.

A beautiful table radio from the early 50's came out with the initial batch. Pat quickly claimed it. It was a Philco AM-FM in the Bakelite plastic of its day, perfectly art deco.

Carol spotted a pair of high-fashioned Armani shoes. "I'll take those shoes no matter what their size might be!" she yelled.

Next was a full box of books. On the top was an edition of "Gone With The Wind." I asked for the whole box and they gladly gave it to me. Some turned out to be first editions and very collectible.

A collapsible liquor bar was dragged off the rear of the truck. Carol screamed and made claim to it quickly. It was made of mahogany and had shelves for storage.

Carol's trusty jeep couldn't have held more. We struggled to pack and unpack these adventurous finds into her car, then onto the ferry, and then into our own vehicles when our trip had finally come to its end. Yes, it was even an experience to unload when reaching home.

As you can see the Nantucket dump was one of the highlights of our special trip to this island paradise.

It is still there folks. On your next trip, or your first one, don't forget the dump. It is highly recommended.

J. C. Nickels, Co.
to Close 39 Stores

The J.C. Nickels Company, (not to be confused with The J.C. Penney Company) of Holy Acre, Vermont has announced the closing of 38 of their top-producing retail stores in the United States. The firm currently operates 134 retail outlets around the world.

Mervin Nickels, great-grandson of Pierre-Wooden Nickels III, who had built the empire of fashionable footwear for left-handed people, and who had been recognized by the footwear industry for his multi-colored shoe-laces and smart-wooden buttons for pierced ears, released this statement to the press on Wednesday.

Mr. Nickels' announcement came after the Board of Directors had considered the lack of increased sales, the world recession, and the unemployment problems here in this country.

The lace business had dropped off some 38 percent, and the left-handed shoe division had seen a decrease in new born left-handers.

The Wooden Pierced Ear Division reported a gain of 31 percent most of which came from their Fall River, Massachusetts outlet.

Mr. Nickels further stated that four stores in Ohio have been sold outright to the SeaThru Bra Company of Upper-Yours, Pennsylvania for some 13 million dollars.

SeaThru President, Howard Goofoff explained the purchase. He stated that they "figured" the sale would help them "round-out" their other locations and it was sure to give an "uplift" to their "sagging" market.

Mr. Nickels said that the closing was to take place in a "quarter" of the time and it was scheduled "to be on the dime."

The writer asked him "for a penny for his thoughts."

I Stole Some Pears...
and Returned Apples

Mr. and Mrs. Nagarian owned a block of real estate on Dunnell Avenue in Pawtucket, Rhode Island where I spent most of my childhood back in 1946.

Mr. Nagarian owned a small department store in downtown and was considered to be quite affluent within the community.

They had built a lovely wooden home on their property and the rest of the land around it was beautifully filled with colorful flowers and several fruit trees.

A healthy pear tree was planted close to the corner of their acreage and the city street closest to my house.

One evening, a group of my young friends spotted the ripe pears and decided to take a few to eat.

They reached up above the lower branches and grabbed a few perfect pieces.

One of the guys decided to climb the small tree and shook it. The tree was totally raped of all of its fruit which now lay on the ground.

My friend, who lived the closest, ran home and brought back empty bags to pick-up the loose pears.

I took a bag myself and filled it to the rim. Later, I gave it to my mother who questioned where it had come from.

I told her it was on the ground at the corner and that others had picked fruit as well. (Although It wasn't exactly a lie, I decided not to tell her the whole story.)

Mom accepted my answer and said that she would cook them and make a delicious fruit dessert for the family.

I went to bed after that, but I couldn't sleep. It was bothering me. I knew that it was not right to do what my friend did and that the pears belonged to the Nagarians, not us.

The next morning, I decided to go to confession at the local Catholic church with my friends.

Father Ron of Saint Mary's listened to my problem in a confessional booth. I told him of my feelings and that I didn't know what to do about it.

He asked, "What would you like to do about it?"

"I'd like to give my share of the pears back to the Nagarians, but I can't because my mother is already cooking them."

Father Ron made a suggestion. "Why don't you consider buying some pears or other fruit and return a bag to them… for forgiveness."

So I did just that. I visited a local market, and although they didn't have pears to purchase, I was able to buy a bag of local apples.

When I rang the front door bell of the Nagarian home, I gathered my words to explain what had been weighing on my conscience.

Fortunately, Mrs. Nagarian came to the door. She graciously accepted my bag of apples saying, "it takes a special person to do what you have done here today. You are exonerated for your part in the happening. I won't forget you coming here and telling me of the actual incident."

With that message, I was relieved of my guilt for being part of that childish activity.

Needless to say, I told my friends about what I had done and I was proud to eventually tell my parents about the whole incident, too.

The motto of this story is that no-one should have to live with the guilt that others created and that you may have been only a slight part of.

And, we must all answer for our own actions.

Popcorn is Best After a Rainstorm

There are so many brands of popcorn. Some are available plain, others with butter, cheese, sugar, vinegar, sour cream, bacon, extra salt, or no-salt.

Some are sold in bags, some in boxes, tins or envelopes. Still others come in plastic garbage can-sized containers.

Your favorite grocery stores have most of these choices. The big department stores get into the act, as well. The movie theatres push it to the limit, and it's not cheap.

Purchased nuggets of corn from the markets can be popped at home. You can heat the nuggets to popping temperature either by microwave, gas or electric oven. Just use a little oil (either cooking oil, peanut oil or even olive oil brands).

Your choice of oils can make a difference in the taste of the corn. It is best served with a napkin in a large bowl.

After it rains, everyone needs a supplemental snack. Popcorn is a dynamite answer for that need. Try it... and say that yours truly told you so.

Maybe this is a corny story (pun intended) but be honest. Didn't this story make you foam at the mouth for this readily available, inexpensive, gem of a snack?

Fact: Did you know that there was not any corn available during the year 1943? Probably not, right? The reason was that all of the colonels were at war.

A Rolls-Royce "Swapped" for Real Estate in New York City

Baron Robert Von See had arrived in New York from Germany.

His family had roots in West Germany where his father and grandfather had controlled a small portion of Hefty Island off the coast of the Bork River near the French border.

When Adolf Hitler took control of Germany, the Von See family left their dominion and moved to the Amalfi Coast in Italy.

They purchased an abandoned castle and restored it to its original condition.

Soon the Italian Government became affiliated with Hitler and fear of the future caused them to move once again. Baron Von See sold his castle and other assets and sailed to the United States.

When he arrived in New York State, he set-up an estate near New Rochelle.

He purchased a 1933 Rolls-Royce four-door Sedan in excellent condition. It had belonged to the chairman of Kaiser Shoe Corporation who had lived in Danbury, Connecticut. The chairman had grown too old to drive or use the beautiful vehicle.

The Baron spent $3,000 to buy it.

Paul Astor, of the famous Astor family, had controlled a large portion of holdings in New York City, including much real estate.

And he was an early auto enthusiast.

Having traveled across the ocean on many visits to Europe, he became infatuated with the special vehicles built in the countries of England, France and Germany.

He brought several back with him to the United States including a limited produced Mercedes-Benz model and several other interesting pieces.

He had started his own collection.

One day he met up with the Baron, who boasted of his precious Rolls-Royce sedan.

"Would you sell it to me?" Paul Astor asked.

"Everything I own can always be bought. But it would have to be a very excellent deal, or just forget it," the Baron responded.

"Would you be interested in some real estate in exchange for the vehicle?" Paul Astor returned.

"What do you have in mind?" the Baron questioned.

"How about a block in New York City?" he offered.

"Get your lawyer and let's draw up the papers. It's a done deal," the Baron immediately countered.

Within a week the deal was completed, without the exchange of any money.

Some fifty years later, the Rolls-Royce (which had been well cared for) had an appraised value of $150,000.

The real estate block was believed to be worth approximately eighteen million dollars.

For Paul Astor and his family, this transaction proved to be a poor decision.

For the Baron Von See estate, it was a spectacular "steal."

The moral of this story is: To LAND a great deal, one should AUTO-matically consider a quick closing when a worthy opportunity presents itself.

Andy Rooney Sends One
Direct from Heaven

It's really quite nice up here. You don't have to dress up, you don't have to shave, and toilet paper isn't available (or needed) anywhere.

Morley Safer, Mike Wallace and I create our usual laughter, and 60 MINUTES IN THE CLOUDS is a sensational success.

Instead of a weekly show, we just keep one show ongoing. There is no time slot and no formal rules to limit us.

We wish you could rig up a way to get our "Stick." Oh well, we can wait till you guys arrive.

Though I do miss my family and some friends.

There is no traffic or constant confusion here like there always was in the daily challenge on Earth.

I don't get ridiculed around this place. They just accept me for who I was. Isn't that nice!

Surprise, money doesn't buy anything around here, either. There are no mortgages to pay, taxes to address or maintenance to consider. We just lean back and float. It is beyond super. You guys don't know what you're missing.

Take it from me. Set you're sights high, be good to your fellow man (or woman), and pray to God. Then we'll be sure to see ya' soon.

Please send me a reply.

Andy Rooney

c/o God

P .S. Dr. Kevorkian sends his regards.

Teddy Roosevelt's Socks

Martha "Mittie" Roosevelt had just purchased a pair of yellow tiger-striped socks, size 14 for her teenage son. Her son Teddy had just turned thirteen. The year was 1871.

She had searched everywhere to find the socks. They were of high-quality and were very colorful to say the least. She had hoped her special son would appreciate them. Only time would tell.

The socks were made of cotton and a nylon substance of the day. They cost his mother $2.83 -- a great sum of money for that time.

Teddy hated the socks but he knew that he had to wear them to appease his mother.

She washed them each week until he left home at age seventeen to enter Harvard College.

Teddy gave the socks to his roommate, John Holcombe.

Holcombe tired of them after several weeks of wearing them and presented them to his sister's boyfriend, Alexander Beers.

Beers donated them to his church bazaar in 1891. The colorful socks were purchased by a Sadie Weinershnitzel for 20 cents.

Sadie used the socks to help display a picture of her late dog "Daffy" who had been killed by a car two years prior. The socks surrounded the picture that graced her fireplace mantle.

Sadie passed away some five years later. Her daughter Bess washed the socks and gave them to her niece Claire who happened to be built like a husky man. The socks fit her comfortably.

Claire ripped the socks and had to sew them back into a useable shape. She wore them for several years before putting them into her trash can for disposal.

The City of Hoboken New Jersey's refuse department had a dozen trucks they used for pick-up for the tax-paying residence's regular weekly trash.

Truck number nine was in use when it approached Claire's house on Upper Washington Boulevard.

Tommy Whitney grabbed her trash bucket and proceeded to empty it into the back of his trusty truck.

The colorful worn socks dropped out to the corner of the truck. Tom quickly pushed them aside, and after emptying the container, took the socks, folded them, and placed them into his outer jacket pocket.

The socks had now changed hands once again.

Tom Whitney washed and wore those socks for some three years. Then he used them to wash his car and clean the windows of his house. It was now his turn to throw them out. He put them with other clothes that had outlived their use. The bag filled up quickly.

The Salvation Army graciously accepted Tom's donation. They were to process the items as usual and bring the saleable pieces to their nearby retail store.

Teddy Roosevelt's tiger sox were still a viable sales item. They were washed and ticketed.

Someone in the Salvation Army's employ had recently studied pictures of former President Theodore Roosevelt and remembered seeing him at about age fifteen wearing socks similar to these newly donated items.

She decided to write a note and attach it to the socks stating, "these socks are duplicates of the socks worn by our late President Teddy Roosevelt during his teenage years."

Sally Ann Scheidgrass, a distant cousin to Richard Nixon, purchased the socks for fifty cents.

Sally was to appear at cousin Richard's 30th birthday party the following week. She thought it might make a great and unusual gift.

Little did she know that Richard was to value her gift and wear them for quite some time.

Many people, to this day, think that Richard might have worn them to his own presidential inauguration.

Teddy's mother would have been very proud if the socks had made their way to this historic event.

The final question, where are these socks today?

Someone ought to submit an ad to the *New York Times* to search for this special item.

It is possible that the socks may be somewhere in the Nixon family today. Will someone please search?

My story ends here.

Stalin Played a "Mean" Clarinet

The Soviet Union tyrant Joseph V. Stalin was not known as a musician. Yet in 1895, at the age of seventeen, he was playing traditional Russian music on a bent and cracked clarinet.

His family and close friends encouraged him to attempt to make a musical career with his instrument. If only he had decided to become an accomplished musician, the world might have been different during those long years of his terrible reign as a dictator.

History tells us that he chose to put aside his clarinet and distance himself from his family. Eventually he joined the revolution and the military.

His rise to power came after Premier Lenin died and a second revolution began.

We cannot correct history.

If "Uncle Joe" (as many called him) had continued with his clarinet skills, he might have become an international star.

He could have played La Scala, Carnegie Hall and even performed with Benny Goodman or Arthur Fiedler. Who knows?

Not much good came from Joseph Stalin.

However, if someone could discover the whereabouts of his old clarinet, it could be worth many, many Russian rubles.

Elizabeth Taylor's Tailor

I'm Tommy Taylor, a tailor by profession. My grandfather and father were both tailors. None of us are related to the famous actress Elizabeth Taylor.

My mother's maiden name was Trouser. Her first name was Beth, but everyone called her Elizabeth.

My dad Preston (Press) Taylor married Elizabeth Trouser and she became Elizabeth (Trouser) Taylor.

I soon became a tailor in training.

We all grew up and lived in the East Hollywood area of California, just a few miles from Los Angeles.

My dad, Press Taylor, would press all the clothes for that famous lady, Elizabeth Taylor.

When I came into the business many years later, I began shortening clothes and fixing zippers for her.

One time I sewed a beautiful artificial flower to the lapel of her newly purchased, expensive suit. I panicked that I may not have completed the work properly.

I guess I did it to her satisfaction because she gave me four more dresses and matching scarfs to clean and press.

When she began dating Michael Todd, the Hollywood Producer, he purchased her a magnificent emerald and diamond broach from Cartier. But they erroneously shipped the special piece to my mother, the other Elizabeth Taylor.

She thought that Dad bought it for her. She was overwhelmed by it and began showing it to friends and relatives. Dad kept telling her that he didn't buy it and that it must be a mistake.

Several days later Cartier found the error and notified the rightful Elizabeth Taylor of their shipping mistake.

Elizabeth decided to visit my mother and to confirm Cartier's erroneous shipment.

My mother, being the proper lady that she was, graciously conveyed the jewelry to the rightful intended recipient.

Ten days later United Parcel Service delivered another package from Cartier.

In the box was a magnificent emerald and diamond broach, with a letter from the newly-married Elizabeth Taylor-Todd.

The letter read:

A woman who is teased with jewelry, she should never be neglected.

The jeweler had another piece that matches my broach perfectly and I purchased it for you.

Please accept this gift as a token of our shared love of exceptional jewelry.

My new husband and I send our very best wishes. We hope that you will wear this piece in good health.

-- Regards, Elizabeth (and Michael) Todd

Because my mother's name was the same as the famous movie star, she was rewarded a priceless jewel.

If my name (the author) had been Tiger Woods, I might have gotten a new set of custom golf clubs, or maybe just a dozen golf-balls. Who knows?

I Gave Birth to Triplets on a Boeing 747

I am Barbara Smithberg from Alpine, Vermont. My husband Pierre works on the Vermont Transit Railroad, as an engineer.

Several months ago, our doctor told us that I was carrying two healthy growing infants and that delivery looked like it would be very normal.

A month before my due date, I decided to visit my mother and sister who live in Denver, Colorado. My

husband thought that the visit would be good for me and my family whom I had not seen in over three years.

After a terrific week in Denver, I had my return flight booked on a non-stop Rural Airlines service from Denver to J. F Kennedy Airport in New York.

Pierre was to pick me up at the New York airport and return us to Vermont. I still had at least twenty days to go before my due date.

Wouldn't you know, my babies wanted to be ahead of schedule. Maybe it was the plane rides that forced the early event. But it was to happen, ready or not.

I broke my water upon lift off from Denver. Needless to say, I was a mess. There was never a thought that I would really deliver this early.

The plane's crew caught wind of the situation and became actively involved in my predicament.

They too couldn't believe what was about to happen on board this flight. But to the best of their ability, they prepared in a hurry.

Sure enough, at 32,000 feet above the Earth, my babies wanted to come out (probably to get frequent-flyer points).

The crew had me lie down in the first-class reclining seat and they asked for help from the passengers.

Donna Pearl Jackson, a nurse-from Prescott, Alabama, came from row 14. Right behind her came Jonathan Post, a third year medical student from North Carolina.

They talked as they worked, preparing hot-water and collecting whatever tools that an airplane might have aboard. They were over supplied with towels and blankets.

They were concerned-that-if something went wrong they might not be prepared. They agreed that they would not wait and that they would just have to do their best.

And so, my babies-came bustling out of my belly. One, two and a surprise… three!

Yes, three baby boys. Wow! Peter, Paul and Patrick were born on this Boeing 747 healthy and crying for their food.

I was excited, relieved and overcome with emotion. Medically I felt quite good.

The two individuals who helped me deliver were thrilled to have played such a role. I could not thank them enough. Also, the airline's staff was terrific and deserved special recognition.

I knew immediately that I was a lucky lady to have been helped by such a knowledgeable team that just happened to be on this flight.

And of course, I was beside myself to think that I now had three babies to mother and raise. And they were calling.

What would their father Pierre say? I hoped he was prepared. He would surely be overwhelmed to hear and see three boys added to our young family.

One at a time I breast fed them and they fell asleep. They were wrapped up in airline blankets.

The captain announced the birth to the rest of the passengers. They clapped and began chatter in both sections. My babies and I became the center of the excitement aboard the plane.

Many of the women and some men asked permission to come forward to see the triplets and to wish us the very best. Several took pictures.

Flight #27 finally landed at J. F. Kennedy Airport some ten minutes early.

Pierre was waiting without knowledge of what had happened. He fainted when he saw me in a wheelchair with the triplets. They had to pick him up off the floor of the arrival room. He quickly came around and stood there, unable to speak.

Then he came forward and kissed my cheek and immediately grabbed two of the infants from me.

He couldn't believe that he had missed the delivery and that he now had three sons in his family.

Pierre asked about the delivery and got assurance that I had come through the experience quite well.

Rural Airlines gave our family a $500 gift for the entertainment created aboard their aircraft. They were pleased that everything came out quite well and that mother and infants were doing great.

The local papers and media wrote the story about the event.

Other airlines wished that this had happened aboard their aircraft.

The Vermont Transit Railroad gave Pierre a twenty-dollar a week raise in pay. He will surely need it.

Pierre beat the expression "three for a dollar." He got twenty.

On the Virgin Islands with a Virgin

The U.S. Virgin Islands sit in the Caribbean. They include the islands of St. Thomas, St. Croix and St. John.

Sixty-six-year-old Fred was loaded with physical problems. His legs, back, stomach and nose were all aching with pain and age.

Fred had tried everything in an attempt to solve his misery.

He visited local doctors and hospitals, he got second opinions from Boston's top physicians, and he even tried holistic approaches, all without much success.

Fred said, "I'm willing to try almost anything."

His friend, Seymour Jones, recommended a trip to the Virgin Islands, with a virgin.

So Fred flew to the Virgin Islands.

And Seymour sent him the virgin.

Her name was Cleopatra Lupino, a beautiful brunette, twenty-three years-old, and a graduate of The Sinclair Lewis Fashion Institute in Fall River, Massachusetts. Her dad owned the Portsmouth Steel Corporation, one of the largest steel companies in the Greater Fall River area.

"She was beautiful. I couldn't handle the situation. I had to send her home," Fred exclaimed. "I'm just not worthy of the desire. I'm truly embarrassed."

After a lonely but lovely week in the islands, Fred came home.

Just the thought of "what could have happened" gave him a new, positive mental approach to his physical problems.

After several months of outdoor physical activities, he was able to minimize the pain and he accepted living with the rest of his ailments.

Fred was thankful that his new positive attitude was able to change his life.

The moral of this story is that men who have problems should consider a week in the Virgin Islands with a Virgin. Check with your local travel agent for availability.

Let's Give Animals Voice Boxes
So They Can Speak

Medical research suggests that doctors could insert voice boxes into baby animals.

Intelligent members of the animal kingdom could then be taught to speak with us in the future.

Why not attempt the trial with a smart dog, like a corgi or a setter?

After the implantation, you could place the animal into a family with a baby human, and let them grow and learn together.

The dog (or other animal) could walk on its rear feet and build its body to stand up, like children do.

Maybe they would become best friends during their education and fit into society. It could happen, but will it?

Supposedly, there is research going on in Africa on this very idea. The media has yet to provide any significant coverage. They could be way ahead in their research.

If this were to happen, maybe "barking" would be a sound of the past.

Can you picture dogs (or other animals) graduating from high school and going on to college to earn degrees? Wow! Or bow-wow!

Dogs and other animals could wear clothes like we do. How about animals wearing walking shoes?

What times we could be living in soon?

The pet food stores and the veterinarians would be losing clients.

Your household pets could become equal members of your family.

It is even possible that someday animals will be driving our vehicles.

They could become champion athletes and spectacular musicians.

Will they work and pay the bills... and taxes?

What about alcohol and drugs? Could they serve in the military?

The future regarding animals could be unlimited. Yet the thought of these possible changes are mindboggling.

As for me, I'll still eat plenty of "Animal Crackers" and play with my granddaughter's teddy bear.

About the Author

A life-long Rhode Islander, Burt was raised in Providence and Pawtucket in a family with a diverse musical presence that inspired him to pursue the piano, trumpet, baritone horn and vocals, and develop a profound love for jazz.

The former owner of several successful businesses throughout New England, Burt is now retired and lives in Cranston, Rhode Island.

Burt is also the author of *Round Newport: Recalling 60 Years of Jazz 'Round Newport, Rhode Island* and *Discovering Newport.*

Made in the USA
Charleston, SC
17 November 2016